Sophie
the Sapphire
Fairy

by Daisy Meadows

illustrated by Georgie Ripper

Join the **Rainbow Magic Reading Challenge!**

Read the story and collect your fairy points to climb the Reading Rainbow online. Turn to the back of the book for details!

This book is worth 5 points.

The Fairyland Palace

Adventure Playground

Tippington Manor

Tippington Town

The Tall Toy Store

Fountain

The Jewel Fairies

To Iola and Amany who love
stories about fairies

Special thanks to
Linda Chapman

ORCHARD BOOKS

First published in Great Britain in 2005 by Orchard Books
This edition published in 2016 by The Watts Publishing Group

3 5 7 9 10 8 6 4 2

© 2016 Rainbow Magic Limited.
© 2016 HIT Entertainment Limited.
Illustrations © Georgie Ripper 2005

HiT entertainment

A CIP catalogue record for this book is available from the British Library.

ISBN 978 1 40834 877 2

Printed in Great Britain

MIX
Paper from
responsible sources
FSC® C104740
FSC
www.fsc.org

The paper and board used in this book are made from wood from responsible sources

Orchard Books
An imprint of Hachette Children's Group
Part of The Watts Publishing Group Limited
Carmelite House, 50 Victoria Embankment, London EC4Y 0DZ

An Hachette UK Company
www.hachette.co.uk
www.hachettechildrens.co.uk

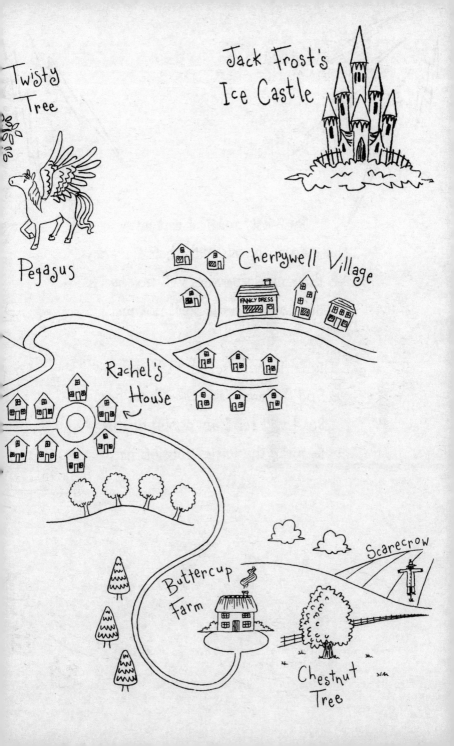

By Frosty magic I cast away
These seven jewels with their fiery rays,
So their magic powers will not be felt
And my icy castle shall not melt.

The fairies may search high and low
To find the gems and take them home.
But I will send my goblin guards
To make the fairies' mission hard.

Contents

Wishes in the Air

"I wish this rain would stop," Kirsty Tate said to her friend, Rachel Walker, as they splashed through the puddles on the busy shopping street. "My trainers are soaked." She pulled the rainbow-coloured umbrella she was holding further down over their heads.

"Mine, too," Rachel said. "Still, I'm glad we came into town today. I got the perfect present for Danny's birthday party next week." She swung the

shopping bag she was holding. It contained a bright red, turbo-charged water pistol that Rachel was sure Danny, her six-year-old cousin, would love.

"I wish I was going to be here for his party," sighed Kirsty.

"Me too. I can't believe you're going home tomorrow," Rachel told her. "This week's gone so quickly."

"Too quickly," replied Kirsty. "I just hope we find another jewel today."

The two girls exchanged a look. They shared an incredible secret. They were best friends with the fairies! They'd helped the fairies out lots of times in the past when nasty Jack Frost had been causing trouble. Now they'd been asked to help again.

This time, Jack Frost had stolen seven magic jewels from Queen Titania's tiara. The jewels controlled special fairy powers and the fairies needed them back so that they could recharge their magic wands. But Jack Frost had banished the jewels to the human world and sent his mean goblin servants to guard them.

Rachel and Kirsty had already helped five of the Jewel Fairies get their magic jewels back, but there were still two gems missing – the Sapphire that controlled wishing magic, and the Diamond that controlled flying magic. Rachel and Kirsty were keen to find them as soon as possible because the fairies' celebration to recharge their wands was supposed to be taking place the very next day!

"We need to find the missing jewels before tomorrow," Kirsty said anxiously. "Maybe we should start looking now."

"But you know what Queen Titania always says," Rachel reminded her.

Kirsty smiled. "Don't look for magic – let it find you," she said.

Rachel nodded. "You're right," she sighed. "We must just wait and see what happens. Let's go this way home," she added, pointing down the street. "We can walk past the mermaid fountain."

"I love the mermaid fountain," Kirsty agreed. "It's so pretty."

The mermaid fountain had a raised circular base with three stone steps leading up to a pool of glittering water. A beautiful stone mermaid and two leaping dolphins had been carved into the fountain. The mermaid's hands were raised above her head and she was holding a large dish.

Water flowed over the sides of the dish and into the pool below.

As Kirsty and Rachel approached they saw a little girl and her mum standing by the fountain.

The girl sighed. "I wish I could have a dolphin of my own, Mum," she said, looking at the dolphins leaping around the mermaid.

The girls heard a faint tinkling sound in the air, and the next moment, a blue balloon came floating down from the sky towards the little girl. Rachel and Kirsty stared in astonishment; the balloon was in the shape of a dolphin!

"A dolphin balloon!" the girl squealed excitedly as she spotted it. "Mum, look!"

Her mum caught the balloon. "Goodness, what a coincidence," she said, looking round to see if anyone had lost it. But the square was empty apart from Rachel and Kirsty. She laughed. "It's almost as if your wish came true, sweetheart!"

Rachel and Kirsty looked at each other. They were both thinking the same thing: could the little girl's wish really have come true?

The girl and her mum hurried off into the rain with the balloon.

"Did you see the way that balloon just appeared out of nowhere?" Kirsty hissed to Rachel.

"Yes. It was just after the little girl said she wished she had a dolphin. Do you think...?" Rachel broke off as a man came walking towards the fountain with a little boy. They were sheltering under an umbrella.

"Can I throw a coin in the fountain
and make a wish, Dad?"
the boy asked.

His dad fished
a penny out of the
pocket of his jeans.
"Tom, catch!" he
said with a grin,
tossing the coin to his son.

Tom caught the shiny penny and ran
up the steps to the pool of water.

"I wish that the rain
would stop so Dad and
I can play football!"
he declared.
As he threw
the penny
into the pool,
water splashed up.

Caught in the air for a moment, the droplets looked like they were glowing and glittering with a magical blue light. Again, the faint tinkle of bells seemed to echo through the air.

As Tom ran down the steps, a ray of sunlight broke through the clouds, lighting up the grey stone of the fountain and making a rainbow in the rain. Then the grey clouds parted overhead and the rain slowly slackened and died away completely.

"It's stopped raining!" Rachel exclaimed, staring up at the sky.

Tom's dad was also looking up in surprise. "What a quick change in the weather!" he remarked.

"It was my wish!" Tom cried. "The fountain must be magic, Dad!"

His dad smiled at him. "Oh, Tom, you know magic isn't real. Come on, let's go home and get the football."

Rachel and Kirsty stared at each other. Whatever Tom's dad might say, they knew the truth: magic was real and wishes could come true. At least, they could if there was a magical fairy Sapphire about.

"Oh, Rachel!" Kirsty gasped as soon as Tom and his dad were out of earshot. "This means Sophie's magic Sapphire must be hidden nearby!"

The Mermaid's Secret

"You're right, Kirsty, the Sapphire must be here somewhere," Rachel said. She glanced around. They were the only people near the fountain now. "Let's have a look."

Kirsty closed the umbrella and put it down on one of the four benches that were placed around the fountain.

She took a quick look underneath the bench, while Rachel peeped behind the bright red pillar box beside it.

"Psst!"

Kirsty and Rachel jumped.

"What was that?" Kirsty asked.

"Psst! Over here!" a silvery voice called softly. Rachel and Kirsty looked around wildly. Where was the voice coming from?

"In the letterbox!" the voice giggled.

Both girls looked at the pillar box.
Sitting in the letter slot,
swinging her legs, was
a very tiny, very
pretty fairy. She
had long, black
shiny hair held
back in a ponytail,
and she was
wearing a short
blue skirt and top.
She waved at the girls.

"Hello, I'm Sophie the Sapphire Fairy,"
she said, smiling. "I've heard how you
helped the other Jewel Fairies. Please
will you help me find my Sapphire?"

"Of course we will," Kirsty
replied eagerly.

"We saw two children making wishes that came true," Rachel told the fairy.

"I know," Sophie replied. "My Sapphire's working its magic. Let's try and find it!"

Rachel began to hunt behind the bench and Sophie zoomed around the pillar box.

"I'll go and look in the fountain," Kirsty called, running up the stone steps.

The bottom of the pool was covered
with turquoise tiles, which
made the water look
really blue. Kirsty
gazed up at the
mermaid statue.
She was even
prettier close
up, but Kirsty
noticed that the
three cherubs
climbing up the
outside of the
mermaid's dish
were the ugliest
cherubs she'd ever
seen. They had
really long noses
and beady eyes.

Suddenly, a flash of blue caught
Kirsty's eye. It seemed to be coming
from just underneath the dish where the
mermaid's hands were. Kirsty peered at
the mermaid's left hand. Then she

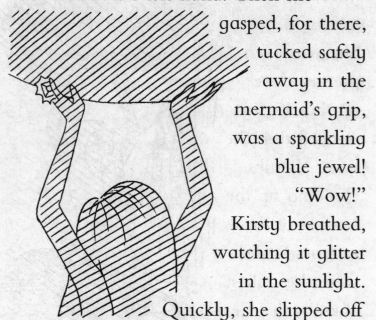

gasped, for there,
tucked safely
away in the
mermaid's grip,
was a sparkling
blue jewel!
"Wow!"
Kirsty breathed,
watching it glitter
in the sunlight.
Quickly, she slipped off
her shoes and rolled up her jeans.

The pool at the base of the fountain
was quite wide but it wasn't very deep.

She could easily paddle across it and reach the statue. She stepped into the water. It was very cold and the tiles felt slippery, but she had to get to the Sapphire. Keeping her eyes firmly fixed on the jewel, Kirsty began to wade through the water.

As she reached the mermaid, her heart pounded with excitement. She stretched up and gently eased the twinkling Sapphire out of the mermaid's fingers. Then she turned to call her friends. "Sophie! Rach—Arghhh!"

She broke off as a blast of water
came shooting at her from one of
the cherubs and hit her straight in
the face.

Spluttering in surprise, Kirsty stared at the cherub. Her eyes widened as she took in its pointy nose, hairy ears and huge feet. It wasn't part of the statue at all. It was one of Jack Frost's horrible goblins!

Kirsty in Trouble

The goblin leapt up onto the top of the dish. "That's my master's jewel!" he shouted. "Put it back right now, pesky girl!"

Kirsty's heart hammered in her chest. To her horror, she saw that there was a second goblin on the fountain also disguised as a cherub – no wonder the

cherubs had looked so ugly. This one
was climbing down towards her with
a mean look on his face.

Kirsty turned to run, but
she was too late. The
approaching goblin
reached out from the
fountain and shoved
her hard in the
chest. Kirsty cried
out as her feet
slipped on the
slimy tiles and
she fell with a splash.
As she landed, the
Sapphire slipped from her
grasp and flew through the air.
It dropped into the pool and sank out
of sight.

Kirsty looked around frantically for the Sapphire, but the tiles of the pool were so bright that she couldn't see the jewel against them. She felt about in the water. Where is it? she wondered. She had to find it before the goblins did. The two goblins jumped down from the fountain and splashed towards her, their beady eyes gleaming. "Stay away!" Kirsty gasped, struggling to her feet. But the goblins began splashing water at her so that she couldn't see a thing.

Coughing and spluttering, Kirsty
scrambled to the edge of the pool. She
was soaked, her hair was dripping and
water was running down her nose.
Rachel came running up the steps with
Sophie flying beside her, the fairy's
silver wings shining in the sun.

"Are you OK?" Rachel cried, helping

Kirsty out of the water. "You're soaking wet and—" She broke off with a gasp as she saw the goblins. "Goblins!"

Kirsty nodded.

"Are you hurt?" Sophie asked anxiously.

"I'm fine, but the Sapphire's in the pool with the goblins," Kirsty replied, shivering. "I found it in the mermaid's hand but then I dropped it."

"You're not getting the Sapphire back!" one of the goblins yelled. "It's ours now." He nudged his companion. "Come on, snail-brain," he ordered rudely. "Hurry up and find it!"

"I don't see why I should do all the work," the other goblin grumbled. He gave the first goblin a shove. "You find it!"

"No, you!" the first goblin yelled, shoving him back.

"Shan't! You do it!"

The water bubbled and foamed as the two goblins pushed each other around the pool, arguing loudly about who should find the jewel.

"We'll never get past those goblins to get to the Sapphire. What are we going to do?" Sophie said, flying to Rachel's shoulder as the two girls retreated down the steps to talk.

"I d—don't know," Kirsty said, her teeth chattering.

"You look freezing," Rachel told Kirsty, taking off her coat. "Have my jacket."

"Thanks," Kirsty said gratefully. "I wish I was warm and dry."

Sophie gave a tinkling laugh. "I can soon sort that out!" she declared. "I've got just enough wishing magic left in my wand for one small wish."

She raised her wand and waved it over
Kirsty's head. Blue and silver sparkles
shot out of the tip and danced in the air.
As they swirled down around Kirsty, a
wave of delicious warmth washed over
her, starting at her head and sweeping
all the way down to her toes.

"I'm dry again!" Kirsty gasped,
looking down at her clothes. "Thanks,
Sophie."

"No problem," replied the little fairy. She flew over and perched on Kirsty's shoulder. "Now, how are we going to get the Sapphire back?"

Kirsty glanced at Rachel. Her friend was staring at the shopping bag on the bench with a thoughtful look on her face. "Rachel?" Kirsty prompted.

Rachel turned to face her friend, her eyes shining. "I've got a plan!" she announced.

Into Battle!

"We'll use the umbrella and the
shopping bag to keep the goblins back
while we search the water for the
jewel," Rachel said eagerly. She saw
puzzled looks on Kirsty and Sophie's
faces. "Sophie, you fly into the air and
drop the shopping bag over the head of
one of the goblins. That will keep him

busy for a while. Kirsty and I can fight
the other goblin off with the umbrella."

"Good plan," Sophie said
approvingly.

"Sounds like I'll be getting wet
again," sighed Kirsty. Then she
grinned. "But I don't care as long as
we get the Sapphire back. Let's do it!"

Rachel took the water pistol out of
the bag while Kirsty
checked that no
one was coming.
"The coast is
clear," Kirsty
reported in
a low voice.
Rachel handed the
bag to Sophie. "Good luck!" she
called as Sophie zoomed into the air.

Then Rachel took a firm hold of the
closed umbrella. "Here goes!" she said,
taking a deep breath and
clutching Kirsty's arm.

Together the girls
ran up the steps
towards the pool.
To their relief they
saw that the
goblins were still
arguing and hadn't
found the Sapphire.

"Slug-brained
nincompoop!" one
of them was shouting.

"Fuzzy-eared idiot!"
the other yelled back.

Holding the umbrella like
a sword, Rachel stepped into the water.

"Arghhh!" she cried to startle the goblins who jumped and squealed in alarm.

Kirsty stamped her feet sending water splashing up around them. At the same moment, Sophie dived down from the sky and dropped the shopping bag neatly over one goblin's head.

"Oi! What's going on?" he yelled, staggering around in the water unable

to see or free his hands. "It's all gone dark!"

Rachel swung the umbrella towards the other goblin. "Quick, Kirsty!" she cried. "Look for the jewel!"

Seeing Kirsty reach down to search for the Sapphire at the bottom of the pool, the goblin began to jump towards the girls, splashing his big feet so that Kirsty couldn't see into the water.

In desperation, Rachel pressed the
button on the umbrella's handle, and
 it suddenly snapped
open to its full size,
fending off the
goblin's splashes.
"Wah!" the
goblin cried,
overbalancing
in surprise.
Meanwhile, Kirsty was feeling
desperately around the pool, searching
for the magic jewel. Her fingers closed
on something smooth and round, and
warm tingles shot up her arm. She
caught her breath. She knew that
feeling; it was fairy magic! "I've got
it!" she cried, pulling the Sapphire from
the water and scrambling to her feet.

But just then Sophie sounded the alarm. "Watch out, girls!" she cried from above.

A jet of water hit Kirsty in the back. She gasped in surprise and whipped round.

A third goblin was standing on the edge of the pool, and in his hands was Danny's turbo-charged water pistol!

Goblin Attack!

"There's another goblin!" Kirsty gasped, remembering that there had been three cherubs on the stone dish. The goblin holding the water pistol must have jumped down from the fountain and sneaked up behind her while she and Rachel were fending off his two goblin friends.

"Give me that jewel!" the goblin yelled. He was bigger than the other two and even scarier, with a long nose and thick eyebrows. He quickly refilled the water pistol from the pool and blasted the girls with another burst of water.

Rachel staggered and dropped the umbrella as the jet of water hit her. "Hey!" she cried, taken aback.

"I want that Sapphire!" the goblin shouted. "And if you don't hand it over, I'll keep shooting at you!"

Sophie darted down from the sky. "Leave Rachel and Kirsty alone, you bully," she cried bravely. "The Sapphire's not yours. It belongs in Queen Titania's tiara!"

"Pesky fairy!" the goblin growled. He lifted his gun and shot water at Sophie,

who squealed in alarm and dodged just in time. The goblin fired again. This time, Sophie only just managed to twist out of the way.

Rachel grabbed Kirsty's arm. "We've got to stop him!" she said anxiously. "If the water hits Sophie it will knock her out of the sky!"

The goblin aimed the water pistol at Sophie again.

"Stop it!" Rachel shouted, wading forwards.

Kirsty followed. "I've got a plan, Rachel!" she hissed. "If we can just reach the edge, maybe we can knock him over. There's only one of him and there's two of us!"

But just then there was a triumphant yell from the middle of the pool. The girls looked round to see that the goblin under the shopping bag had managed to wriggle free. His goblin companion had grabbed the umbrella that Rachel had dropped in all the confusion. All three goblins grinned.

"You won't get away with the Sapphire now!" the goblin with the umbrella said nastily as he began to splash across the pool. The goblin clutching the water pistol stepped into the water and began to wade towards the girls too. "We're trapped!" exclaimed Kirsty, seeing goblins on all sides. "Quick!" Sophie cried from high above. "There are people coming down the street. They'll see what's happening!

We have to get out of here with the
Sapphire!"

Sapphire! The word seemed to burst
into Kirsty's mind. Of course! Why
hadn't she thought of it
before? She was holding
a magic jewel full of
wishing magic! She
looked at the
advancing goblins.
Could she use it to
stop them? Hoping
desperately that her
plan would work, she
lifted the sparkling stone
and cried, "I wish…" she
glanced around for inspiration, and her
gaze fell on the mermaid's tail. "I wish,
I wish you goblins were fish!"

Blue and silver sparks shot into the air. As they streamed down over the goblins' heads there was a tinkling sound and suddenly the three goblins vanished.

"Where have they gone?" Rachel asked. She looked down at the pool. "Oh!"

Kirsty stared into the water. Three goldfish were swimming around her feet. They looked just like ordinary

orange goldfish except that they had
extra-long pointed noses, and very
beady eyes! "The Sapphire worked!"
she breathed.

"Of course it worked," Sophie cried,
swooping down with a silvery laugh.
"It's a wishing jewel, isn't it? It was a
brilliant idea to use it like that, Kirsty!"

"Thanks," Kirsty said, smiling with
relief. She bent down
towards the water.
"I hope you'll be very
happy living here, little
goblin-fish," she said
cheerfully. The fish
darted irritably about
her feet and Kirsty could
have sworn they had
grumpy frowns on their faces.

Giggling, the girls picked up the water pistol, umbrella and shopping bag and climbed out of the fountain.

"Just in time," Sophie said, settling on Rachel's shoulder and hiding under her hair as a group of shoppers entered the square.

The girls sat down hurriedly on one of the benches and tried to look as if they were just chatting normally. Luckily, nobody seemed to notice that they were dripping wet.

As soon as the people had left the square, Sophie peeped out from Rachel's hair. "Thanks for getting the Sapphire back," she said happily.

"That's OK," said Rachel, shivering on the bench. She looked at the sparkling jewel in her hand. "It's beautiful!"

"I know," Sophie smiled. She touched her wand to the surface of the gem and blue sparks flew up. "And now that my wand is full of wishing magic again," she added, waving it in the air to leave a trail of blue and silver glitter, "is there anything you two would like to wish for?"

Kirsty and Rachel looked at each other. "We wish we were warm and dry again!" they chorused.

"Easy!" Sophie declared with an expert wave of her wand. Sparkles swirled around the girls, and within a second their wish was granted.

"Thanks, Sophie," Rachel said gratefully, feeling much warmer now.

"Will the goblins be OK as goldfish?" Kirsty asked.

"They'll be fine," Sophie assured her.

"When Jack Frost learns that the Sapphire's been returned to Fairyland he'll come and find them. That's when they'll be in trouble!"

She touched her wand to the Sapphire as it sat in Kirsty's hand and the girls blinked as it vanished in a fountain of blue sparkles.

"It's safe in Fairyland now," Sophie said. "And I'd better follow it. Goodbye girls, and thank you for saving another of our magic jewels." With that, Sophie flapped her wings, but to Kirsty and Rachel's surprise she didn't actually fly into the air. They saw a look of

concern cross Sophie's face. She
flapped her wings again. Nothing
happened.

"My wings aren't working!" Sophie
exclaimed in complete astonishment.

"What do you mean?" Kirsty asked.

"They won't lift me into the air,"
Sophie replied, looking panicky.

Kirsty looked at the fairy's back.
Sophie's silvery wings looked strangely
faint. "Your wings look really pale,
Sophie," she said.

"Yes, almost see-through," Rachel agreed. "As if they're... well, fading away."

"Fading away!" Sophie exclaimed. "But they can't be!" She stared at the girls in horror. "What's happening? Why can't I fly?"

Fairy Dust

"Maybe you're just tired," Rachel suggested hopefully. "You had to dart about a lot to avoid the water pistol."

Sophie shook her head. "Fairies' wings don't fade when they get tired," she replied. Silvery tears filled her eyes. "I think I must be ill."

"Or perhaps…" Kirsty said, thinking

hard, "...it's got something to do with the missing Diamond."

"Oh, yes, the Diamond!" Rachel echoed. "It's the only jewel we haven't found yet."

Kirsty nodded. "Doesn't the Diamond control flying magic, Sophie?"

"Yes," Sophie agreed.

"Well, maybe the fairies' flying magic is running low because the Diamond is still lost," Kirsty suggested. "It might not be only your wings that are fading, Sophie, it might be all the fairies' wings!" Sophie looked like she didn't know whether to be relieved or even more worried.

"Oh, goodness, I think you might be right, Kirsty!" she gasped. "Our flying magic must be running out!"

"We'll find the Diamond," Kirsty told her quickly. "Don't worry about that, Sophie. But how are you going to get home to Fairyland now?"

"I don't know," replied Sophie, looking troubled. "How can I get back without wings?"

"I've got an idea," Rachel said. "We could use some of our fairy dust!"

"Oh, yes!" Kirsty agreed. She reached into the neck of her T-shirt and pulled out a golden locket. Rachel had a matching one.

"Queen Titania gave us these lockets," she told Sophie. "They're full of fairy dust for us to use if ever we need to get to Fairyland."

"And there's no reason why the fairy dust wouldn't work on a fairy, is there?" Rachel asked Sophie.

"No," cried Sophie. "In fact, I'm sure it would take me straight back to Fairyland."

"Well, here goes…" Kirsty said, opening her locket and taking out a pinch of fairy dust.

"Thanks for all your help, girls," Sophie declared. "I'll be sure to tell everyone how kind you've been."

Very gently Kirsty sprinkled the dust over Sophie's head.

"Goodbye, Sophie!" she and Rachel said together.

The dust swirled around the tiny fairy and Sophie smiled. "It's working. I can feel it. I'm off to Fairyland!" she called, and with a happy wave she disappeared.

"Phew," Kirsty said, in relief. "At least Sophie's safely back home."

"Yes," Rachel agreed happily. "And so is the Sapphire." Standing up, she put the water pistol back into the shopping bag and picked up the umbrella. "It's been an exciting day."

"Almost too exciting," said Kirsty, looking at the fountain. "But at least there's only one jewel left for us to find now."

"But we've got to find it as soon as possible," Rachel pointed out. "The fairies need their flying magic back."

Kirsty nodded in agreement. It was awful to think of all their friends unable to fly. "We'll find the Diamond!" she declared firmly. "Even Jack Frost won't be able to stop us."

Rachel nodded and grinned. "Watch out, goblins. Here we come!"

Now Rachel and Kirsty must help...

Lucy the Diamond Fairy

Read on for a sneak peek...

Kirsty Tate folded her jumper and put it into her bag. "There," she said to her best friend Rachel Walker. "I'm all packed." She looked at the clock on Rachel's bedroom wall. "Six o'clock already!" Kirsty groaned. "Mum and Dad will be here to pick me up soon. I can't believe this week is nearly over, can you?"

Rachel shook her head. "No," she replied. "It's gone so quickly. But it's been great fun."

The girls grinned at one another. Whenever they were together, the two of them always had the most wonderful adventures: fairy adventures! This week, while Kirsty had been staying with Rachel's family for half-term, the girls had been helping the Jewel Fairies find the seven missing magic jewels from Fairy Queen Titania's tiara!

Mean Jack Frost had stolen the gems, and, without them, some very important kinds of fairy magic were running low. So far, Kirsty and Rachel had found six of the stolen jewels – but the Diamond was still to be found.

Kirsty frowned. "I can't help feeling that something's wrong, today," she said. "I was sure we'd find the magic Diamond before I had to go home."

"Me, too," Rachel agreed. "And we haven't even seen a fairy yet. I wonder if they're all trapped in Fairyland."

The girls exchanged worried glances. They both knew that the Diamond controlled flying magic, and while it was missing, the fairies were starting to lose their ability to fly. The last fairy they'd seen, Sophie the Sapphire Fairy, had actually found her wings fading by the end of the day.

"We'll just have to find the Diamond and send it safely back to Fairyland by ourselves," Kirsty said in a determined voice. "Do you think we should start looking?"

Before Rachel could reply, both girls heard a delicate tinkling sound.

"It's your jewellery box," Kirsty said in surprise. "It's playing a tune all by itself!"

The girls rushed over to the jewellery

box on Rachel's chest of drawers. Kirsty had one just the same at her house; they'd been presents from the Party Fairies. To anybody else, the jewellery boxes looked ordinary enough. Only Kirsty and Rachel knew that they had been made with a sprinkling of magical fairy dust.

"Listen," Rachel hissed. "I can hear singing!"

Both girls strained their ears to hear the faint sweet voices floating out of the jewellery box.

Just as abruptly as it had started, the music stopped with a click.

Rachel's eyes were wide. "If the Diamond's in Fairyland, we need to be there too," she said.

Kirsty nodded and quickly opened the

locket that she always wore around her neck. Queen Titania had given the girls matching lockets full of fairy dust which would take them straight to Fairyland if ever they needed help. "Let's use our last pinches of fairy dust to get there," she suggested...

Read Lucy the Diamond Fairy to find out what adventures are in store for Kirsty and Rachel!

Meet the Jewel Fairies

Join Rachel and Kirsty as they hunt for the
jewels that naughty Jack Frost has stolen
from Queen Titania's crown!

www.rainbowmagicbooks.co.uk

Calling all parents, carers and teachers!
The Rainbow Magic fairies are here to help
your child enter the magical world of reading.
Whatever reading stage they are at, there's
a Rainbow Magic book for everyone!
Here is Lydia the Reading Fairy's guide to
supporting your child's journey at all levels.

Starting Out

Our Rainbow Magic Beginner Readers are perfect for first-time readers who are just beginning to develop reading skills and confidence. Approved by teachers, they contain a full range of educational levelling, as well as lively full-colour illustrations.

1

Developing Readers

Rainbow Magic Early Readers contain longer stories and wider vocabulary for building stamina and growing confidence. These are adaptations of our most popular Rainbow Magic stories, specially developed for younger readers in conjunction with an Early Years reading consultant, with full-colour illustrations.

2

Going Solo

The Rainbow Magic chapter books - a mixture of series and one-off specials - contain accessible writing to encourage your child to venture into reading independently. These highly collectible and much-loved magical stories inspire a love of reading to last a lifetime.

3

www.rainbowmagicbooks.co.uk

"Rainbow Magic got my daughter reading chapter books. Great sparkly covers, cute fairies and traditional stories full of magic that she found impossible to put down" - Mother of Edie (6 years)

"Florence LOVES the Rainbow Magic books. She really enjoys reading now" Mother of Florence (6 years)

The Rainbow Magic Reading Challenge

Well done, fairy friend – you have completed the book!
This book was worth 5 points.

See how far you have climbed on the **Reading Rainbow**
on the Rainbow Magic website below.

The more books you read, the more points you will get,
and the closer you will be to becoming a Fairy Princess!

How to get your Reading Rainbow
1. Cut out the coin below
2. Go to the Rainbow Magic website
3. Download and print out your poster
4. Add your coin and climb up the Reading Rainbow!

There's all this and lots more at
www.rainbowmagicbooks.co.uk

You'll find activities, competitions, stories, a special
newsletter and complete profiles of all the
Rainbow Magic fairies. Find a fairy with your name!